MARIE CURIE
A LIFE OF DISCOVERY

ALICE MILANI

TRANSLATION BY
KERSTIN SCHWANDT

Graphic Universe™ • Minneapolis

Scientific consultants: Anna Nobili and Andrea Milani

First American edition published in 2019 by Graphic Universe™

Published in arrangement with AMBook (www.ambook.ch)

Translation by Kerstin Schwandt

Graphic Universe™
An imprint of Lerner Publishing Group, Inc.
241 First Avenue North
Minneapolis, MN 55401 USA

For reading levels and more information, look up this title at www.lernerbooks.com.

Photo credits: Hulton Archive/Getty Images, p. 202; Wikimedia Commons (public domain), p. 203.

Main body text set in Skippy Sharp 14/14. Typeface provided by Chank.

Library of Congress Cataloging-in-Publication Data

Names: Milani, Alice, 1986- author, illustrator. | Schwandt, Kerstin, translator.
Title: Marie Curie : a life of discovery / Alice Milani ; translation by Kerstin Schwandt.
Other titles: Marie Curie. English
Description: First American edition. | Minneapolis : Graphic Universe, [2019]. | Originally published: [Padua] : BeccoGiallo, 2017. | Audience: Ages 14-18. | Audience: Grades 9 to 12. | Includes bibliographical references.
Identifiers: LCCN 2018038300 (print) | LCCN 2018056938 (ebook) | ISBN 9781541561137 (eb pdf) | ISBN 9781541528178 (lb : alk. paper)
Subjects: LCSH: Curie, Marie, 1867-1934—Comic books, strips, etc. | Curie, Marie, 1867-1934—Juvenile literature. | Women physicists—Poland—Biography—Comic books, strips, etc. | Women physicists—Poland—Biography—Juvenile literature. | Women physicists—France—Biography—Comic books, strips, etc. | Women physicists—France—Biography—Juvenile literature. | Women chemists—Poland—Biography—Comic books, strips, etc. | Women chemists—Poland—Biography—Juvenile literature. | Women chemists—France—Biography—Comic books, strips, etc. | Women chemists—France—Biography—Juvenile literature. | Women Nobel Prize winners—Biography—Comic books, strips, etc. | Women Nobel Prize winners—Biography—Juvenile literature.
Classification: LCC QD22.C8 (ebook) | LCC QD22.C8 M5413 2019 (print) | DDC 540.92 [B]—dc23

LC record available at https://lccn.loc.gov/2018038300

Manufactured in the United States of America
1-44698-35531-12/26/2018

For Alessandro

Oh we
who wished to set the stage for kindness
could not ourselves be kind

—Bertolt Brecht, "To Those Who Follow in Our Wake," 1939

PARIS, 1936
Ève?
He's arrived.
Tell him I'll be right down.
Paris
Paris

Very well.
My sister will be down in a moment.
Thank you.
May I offer you a cup of tea?
No thank you, Madame Irène.
Please don't trouble yourself.

SZCZUKI, EAST-CENTRAL POLAND, 1889
THE ŻORAWSKI RESIDENCE
Tell me everything about Warsaw. How are your classes at the university?

Well, Mother . . .
The professor of agriculture really likes me.
May I come in?

Come, Manya!
KASIMIERZ!

OH, KAZIK!!
This is Maria, our new housekeeper.
Oh, she's exquisite!
She even speaks French.
She's just finished her studies in Warsaw. With honors!
Bring Anja out too, if she's finished her homework.
Right away, Madame Żorawski.

She seems nice.
Oh, come on up here, you.
That poor girl—what an unfortunate family.
What?
Oof . . .
Where to begin?
Maria's father is out of work. Her mother died of tuberculosis . . .
It's a tragedy.

Her father, Władysław, was the headmaster of a school until not long ago.
They're educated people.
But...
With all these restrictions in place, because of these tsarists...
All the lessons have to be in Russian and Polish is prohibited and so on...
He resisted, they caught him, and bang! They kicked him out.
Hm.
Good night, mother!
Where are you going?

Knock
Knock
Je voudrai.
s...
Que tu arreté.
Arrêtais.
Ugh!
But they're pronounced exactly the same!
Yes, Anja, but you need the circumflex accent.
May I come in?
...

So you're from Warsaw.
I go to university there.
Lucky you.
And you?
What are you studying?
Ah, French!
Anja, go get a glass of water.
The young lady must be thirsty after all this work, yes?
Go on.

My dear sister Bronya, if you only knew how I long to go to Warsaw, if only for a few days . . . Let's not even speak about the state of my clothes—but my soul too is worn out.

Ah, if I could leave this icy atmosphere for just a few days . . .
Sit down, Anja!
Asseyez-vous.
La fourchette!
The constant control I must keep over my words, my expression, my movement . . . it wears me out.
Anja! Get your elbows off the table!
If a man's family won't let him marry a poor governess, well, he can go to hell! Besides, nobody asked him to.
You may leave, dear.

But why pile on? Why upset an innocent soul?
Good night, Madame.
My plans for the future?
I have none.
Or rather, they are too commonplace and simple to mention.

If I ever had any others, they have gone up in smoke.
I have buried them.
Locked them up.
Sealed and forgotten them.

My little Manya, you must make something of your life.
If you can manage to save a few hundred rubles this year, you can come and live with us in Paris next year. I guarantee that in two years you will have your master's degree.
Now is your time to decide. You have been waiting too long.

Think about it. You can't waste your gifts on a man who will not marry you.
And you have gifts. I know it.

Bronya!
Manya!
NORD
NORD
How was the trip?
Eh...
Long!

PARIS, 1891
BRASSERIE LE DOME

Let us determine the condition by which the simple integral

$$\int(A_1 dx_1 + A_2 dx_2 + \ldots + A_n dx_n)$$

is an integral invariant with respect to closed lines.

Let us carry out the change in variables as indicated above, and our integral will become

$$\int(B_1 dy_1 + B_2 dy_2 + \ldots + B_{n-1} - dy_{n-1} + B_n dz),$$

which I can write again, taking the most symmetrical notation from the end of the preceding section

$$\int \sum B_i dx'_i.$$

However, the integral of the second member of
$\int\sum B_i dx'_i = \int\sum(dB_i/dx'_k - dB_k/dx'_i)\, dx'_i dx'_k$
must be an absolute integral invariant . . .
Psst!
Did you find out where she's from?
She didn't tell me, but I think she's German.
And not only with respect to the closed subsets.
SCRIB SCRIB SCRIB SCRIB

We can therefore conclude the following: In order that ∫ΣB dx be an integral invariant with respect to the closed lines . . .
Then what did you talk about? Can't you tell me anything?
Not really, I didn't . . .
SHHHHH!!!
it is necessary and sufficient that the binomials dB/dx' − dB/dx' all be independent of z.
Shh!
Similarly, and more generally, ∫ΣAdω be an integral expression of the order p . . .
Entschuldigung, Fräulein!
. . .
. . . Having the same form as those that were discussed in the preceding sections.
The perfect student! Be careful, pretty German girl! Studying too hard will ruin your eyes!
Heh heh! You'll turn into a hunchback, and then how will you find a husband?

Tsk.

"Pretty German girl."

6
LETTRES

Idiots . . .
6
LETTRES

* What is it?

** Put your hand here.

*** Will this take long?

**** I have cakes in the oven.

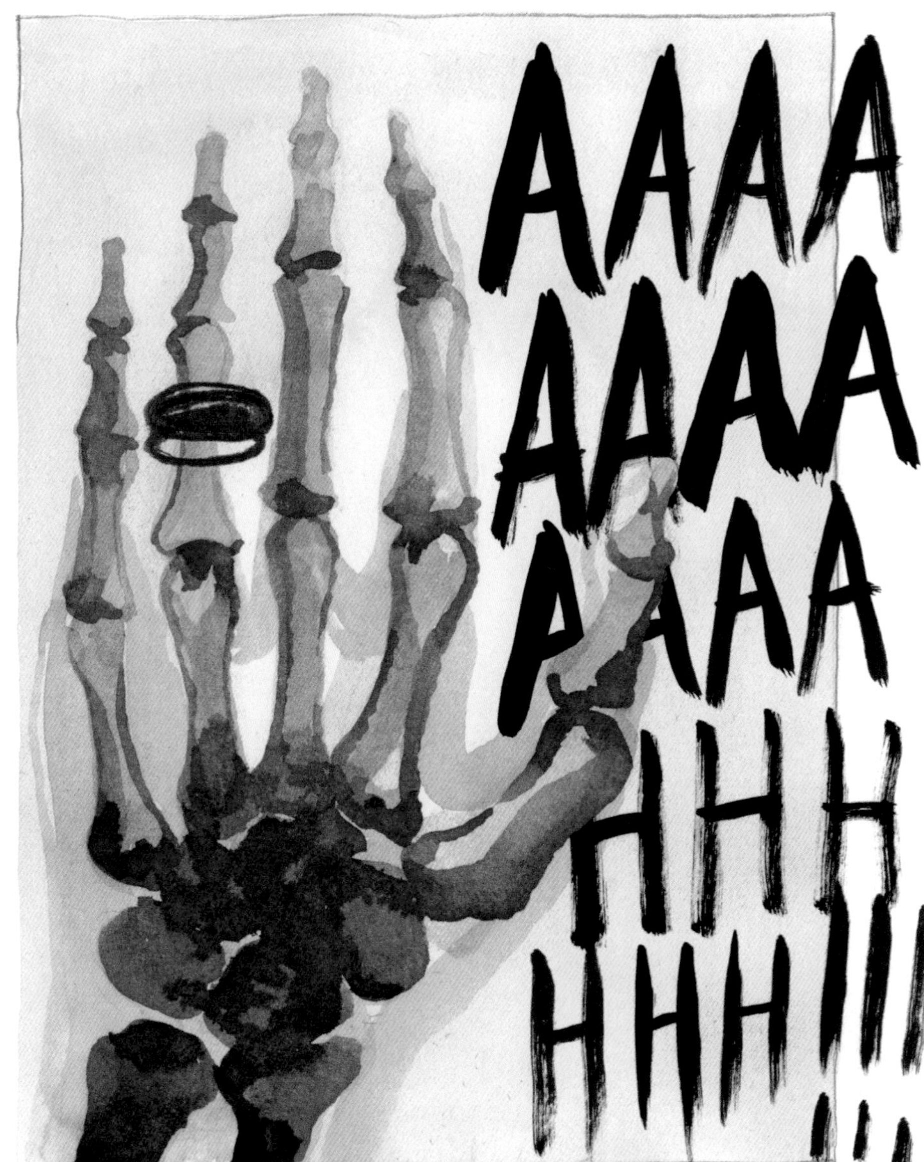

* Hold still.

** How did it come out?

knock
knock
Coming!
SPRING 1894
Marie!
Come in.
Your sister's already here.
Manya!
Hi, Bronya.
How are you, dear?
You look a little exhausted!
No, no, I'm fine!
How are your classes going?
Oh, good . . .
Here, give me your scarf.
Marie!
Come here!
I must introduce you to someone.

Pierre,
my dear colleague!

This is Marie.
Marie Skłodowska, in her final year at the Sorbonne—she's quite a talented student.
She's doing research on
The first time I saw Pierre, I noticed. . .
. . . in the Sorbonne laboratory. Maybe you two can talk a little bit, eh?
Pleased to meet you.
He works at the School of Physics and Industrial Chemistry. He can help you.
The pleasure is mine.
Right, Pierre?
Anyway, listen, he's a very good physicist and a fantastic person!
Now, if you'll excuse me, my wife wants me.
That's a handsome man.

So. Marie Sk . . .
Skłodowska.
It's Polish.
And you're at the Sorbonne?
A grave and gentle expression on his face, and perhaps an air of melancholy . . .
I'm going to get a degree.
In mathematics.
I have one in physics.
This will be my second.
Oh!
Hmm, interesting!

And what...
A-ahem.
?
Excuse me.
And...
As I was saying—what are you working on?
Oh, on certain steels...
...and their different reactions to magnetic fields.
Oh, interesting!
But...

* École supérieure de physique et de chimie industrielles, the School of Physics and Industrial Chemistry

Thank you.
You're walking quietly down the street...
And someone with X-ray glasses...
ZAP!!
HAHA
AHAHA
HAHA
HA
HAHA
HAHA
...Can see under your skirt!
HA HAHA HAHA
HA H
HEE HEE
Madness, right?
You two have read it too, yes?
Are you talking about the rays discovered by that German,
Röntgen?

They can see through flesh.
It's like witchcraft, Marie!
What are you talking about, Dłuski?
Are you getting this from the newspapers?
There will surely be an explanation.
We just haven't gotten there yet.
Look at today's edition.
I have it right here. Read it!
Who writes these articles?
Jackals . . .
LE JOURNAL
X-RAYS
Scientific Phenomenon or
Paranormal?
Experts react

COF! COF!
ECOLE DE PHISIQUE ET DE CHIMIE INDUSTRIELLE
Marie. Good morning.
Hello, Pierre.
Shall we go in?
E.P.C
Pierre?
Hey, Paul.
Pierre!
I have a favor to ask, my friend . . .

Miss, permit me just a moment . . .
But what—
Pierre . . .
What's going on?
You need to hold on to these 200 francs for me.
What?
Please, don't ask any questions.
It's to keep them away from Jeanne. If she finds them in the house, she'll take them.
Paul!
Did you have another fight?
We've . . . reached an impasse.
Uh . . . ?
Is everything all right?
Oh, yes!
That was nothing.
Let's go this way.
Who is he?
Bye, Paul!
That's Paul Langevin.

He was my student, then my colleague.
He's a good physicist. And a friend.

After you...
Oh!
This is your laboratory?
It's a little small, but anyway, yes. It's my space.
What are you working on?
Crystals. For many years now.

My brother Jacques and I have discovered that if we apply pressure . . .
On certain types of crystals . . .
The structure of the crystal is deformed.
The two sides are polarized.
An electric potential difference is created.
All charges align themselves . . .
As if they were combed.
I'm convinced that it's because the structure is asymmetric.
I've made drawings where—
And you managed to measure it?
What?
The potential difference.

We have developed this instrument . . .
Here inside there's a quartz crystal.
You put the weights here?
Yes.
Under the pressure of the weight, the crystal emits a charge. Then a classic quadrant electrometer measures it.
Nice!
So your brother is also a scientist?
Yes.
What about you? Do you have brothers?
Yes, one, named Józef. And another sister, Helena, in Warsaw.

But my elder sister, Bronya, who you met, lives here in Paris with her husband.
You don't live with her?
Oh no!
I rented a room nearby. I can work much harder that way.
You saw what kind of brother-in-law I have.
With him in the house, it's always a party! I couldn't get any studying done.
Would you like to . . .
I don't know, have something to eat? Together?
Oh! Now?
I mean, tonight?
Sure . . .
Well. Why not?

Was it hard in the beginning?
The courses at the Sorbonne, I mean.
Well, there were big gaps while I was a housekeeper, trying to study on my own. That was difficult.
Also, I didn't have a laboratory.
Right.
I understand.
So...
CAREFUL!!
Sorry!

Pierre!
For goodness' sake . . .
Pay attention!
You're right.
I'm so distracted . . .
As I was saying . . .
What would you like to do after you graduate?
I'm going back to Poland. Naturally.
I can contribute to the cause of social progress through the education of the masses! You know, in Warsaw . . .
Students have created a network of clandestine classes. They call it the Flying University.
It's a very ambitious project, and it's of the utmost importance to the country!
Table for two?

My people are risking prison for something bigger than themselves.
The Russians, who dominate my homeland, would throw them in jail without thinking twice if they knew that they held lessons in Polish!
My cousin . . .
He's a chemist.
He was a student of Mendeleev in Petersburg. He's secretly forming a society of young people.
They will be the scientists and intellectuals of a liberated Poland.
You can't hope for a better world without first improving individuals.
Don't you agree?
Marie . . .

You can't change the social order like that.
Not overnight.
Think about it.
These mechanisms are too complex for anyone to understand completely.
Let alone change.
From a scientific point of view, however, we can do something.
There's a foundation to build on.
And every discovery will be a step forward.
We can really make progress here.

Marie . . .
You must do research.
Stay here in Paris.
You don't understand!
I owe it to my father.
My sisters.
My country.
Ah, yes . . .
You're right.
Who am I to tear you away from your beloved Poland?

WARSAW,
SUMMER 1894
Pierogi

My dear friend Marie, nothing would please me more than to hear from you.
PARA
SOU
24

I would be very happy if you return my letters and assure me that you're coming back in October.
Papa!
I know that my nagging irritates you, so I won't say much more.

I showed a picture of you to my brother. I hope you don't mind?
He thinks you're beautiful.
So what do you think of that little apartment on Rue Mouffetard?
Do you want to rent it with me?
He also said you have a determined, stubborn expression.

It has windows over the courtyard.
...
We don't need to rush things, Pierre.
We can start by sharing the laboratory.
TERMINUS NORD
Brasserie

And after sharing the laboratory for
a year, Pierre and I got married.
The thought of spending all my life
in Paris pains me. Far away from my
beloved Poland, and far away
from Papa . . .
But what can I do?
Destiny has bound us so
permanently that we can't
bear the idea of being apart.

PARIS, 1936
This is you?
With your mother?
Yes.
And here?
Where were you?

On a boat to the United States. My mother lectured at a series of conferences.
This is Ève?
Yes.
And this is you.
That's remarkable!

The resemblance. You know what I mean?

Hm.

Do you see it?

Knock knock
Henri?
May I come in?
Sure, come in!
PARIS, 1896
Henri.
I must talk to you.
Go ahead, Becquerel.
Considering the profound esteem and friendship that binds us . . .
What's wrong?
I would never permit myself to disturb you if it wasn't . . .
For an unprecedented, inexplicable case . . .
That fills me with dismay!
As you can see, the signs are clear.
Oh God!
What is this?
I don't understand!
SBAM!
Rays that can pass through matter!

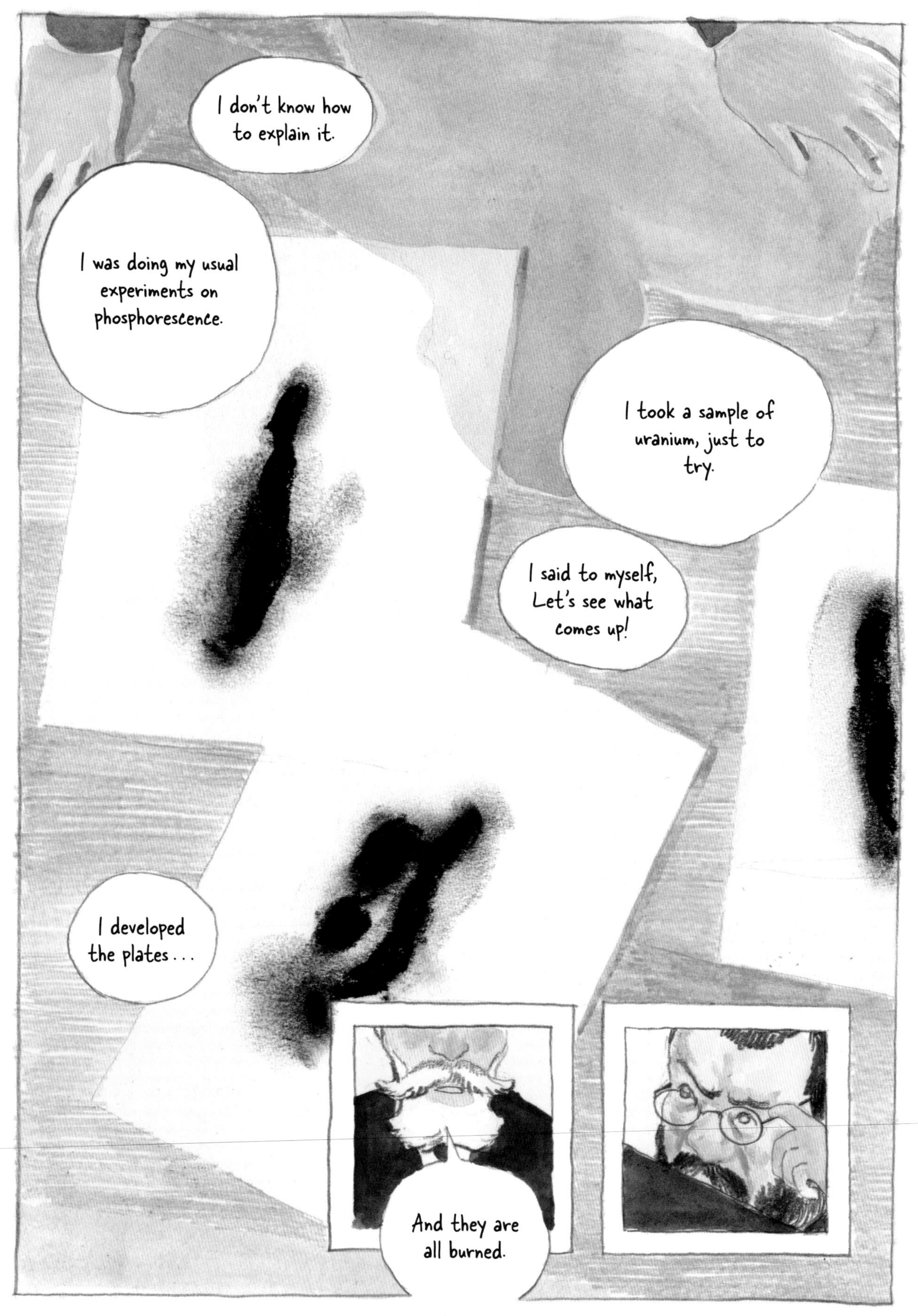
I don't know how to explain it.
I was doing my usual experiments on phosphorescence.
I took a sample of uranium, just to try.
I said to myself, Let's see what comes up!
I developed the plates . . .
And they are all burned.

Here's what I did:

I took a photographic plate with a bromide emulsion and wrapped it in two sheets of thick, black paper. Completely protected from the sunlight.

I placed a layer of uranium salts on the outside of the envelope.

I left it in the sun for four hours.

Then I developed the plate . . .

And see?

The rays crossed through the paper! And they made an impression on the plate.

Hmm . . . interesting.
It's like Röntgen's X-rays.
No, Poincaré.
There's a big difference.
Röntgen used a very high-voltage electric current . . .
To inject energy into the vacuum tube.
Then, of course, some electrons would hit the wall of the tube and . . .
BAM!!
Because of the sudden impact . . .
X-rays were produced. Invisible but highly penetrating.

But this is something different.
I didn't do anything to trigger all of this.
Maybe the sun's rays charged the uranium salts . . .
No!
It can't be.
Listen to this: I conducted the same experiment with a clean photographic plate. I covered it in the same way, put the same uranium salts on it . . .
But without exposing the covered plate to sunlight.
It produced the same photographic impressions.
In the dark?
Yes.
Shut away for three days in a dra

Hm.

Strange.

But I assume the phenomenon would weaken after a while, right?

scratch scratch

Perhaps it's just another type of phosphorescence that lasts longer than the others.

I'M TELLING YOU, NO! NOT EVEN KEEPING THE SALTS IN THE DARK STOPS IT!!

!!?

Are you trying to say that uranium emits spontaneous rays? Without any kind of external stimulation?

So then it's no longer a phenomenon of phosphorescence.

This is not an energy that's accumulated and then emitted later.

BUT THEN WHAT IS IT??

We are on the verge of a PHENOMENON of a completely different ORDER
"Mama."
Say "Mama."
PA PA PA PAA
Not "Papa."
"Mama"!
PA!
Oh my God, look how much you did, Irène!
Here, I'm going to change you now.
Www . . .
Pierre—
Did you read . . .
WHAAA!

What did you say, honey?
Did you read this Becquerel article?
BA!
He describes rays emitted by uranium . . .
That can pass through matter.
I've been thinking about it for a while.
Now I've made a decision.
I'd like to do my thesis on it.
I think that's a great idea!
You know it's a new phenomenon, those rays. Nobody has ever studied it.
Say . . . will you lend me your instrument with the quartz?
Perfect.
What are you going to do?

Measure of radiation from a sample = measure of air conductivity under the effect of the active substance

Humid day.

Possible increase in air conductivity.

Cough cough!
Six degrees Celsius!
(In the laboratory, not outside.)
I could build a plate condenser . . .

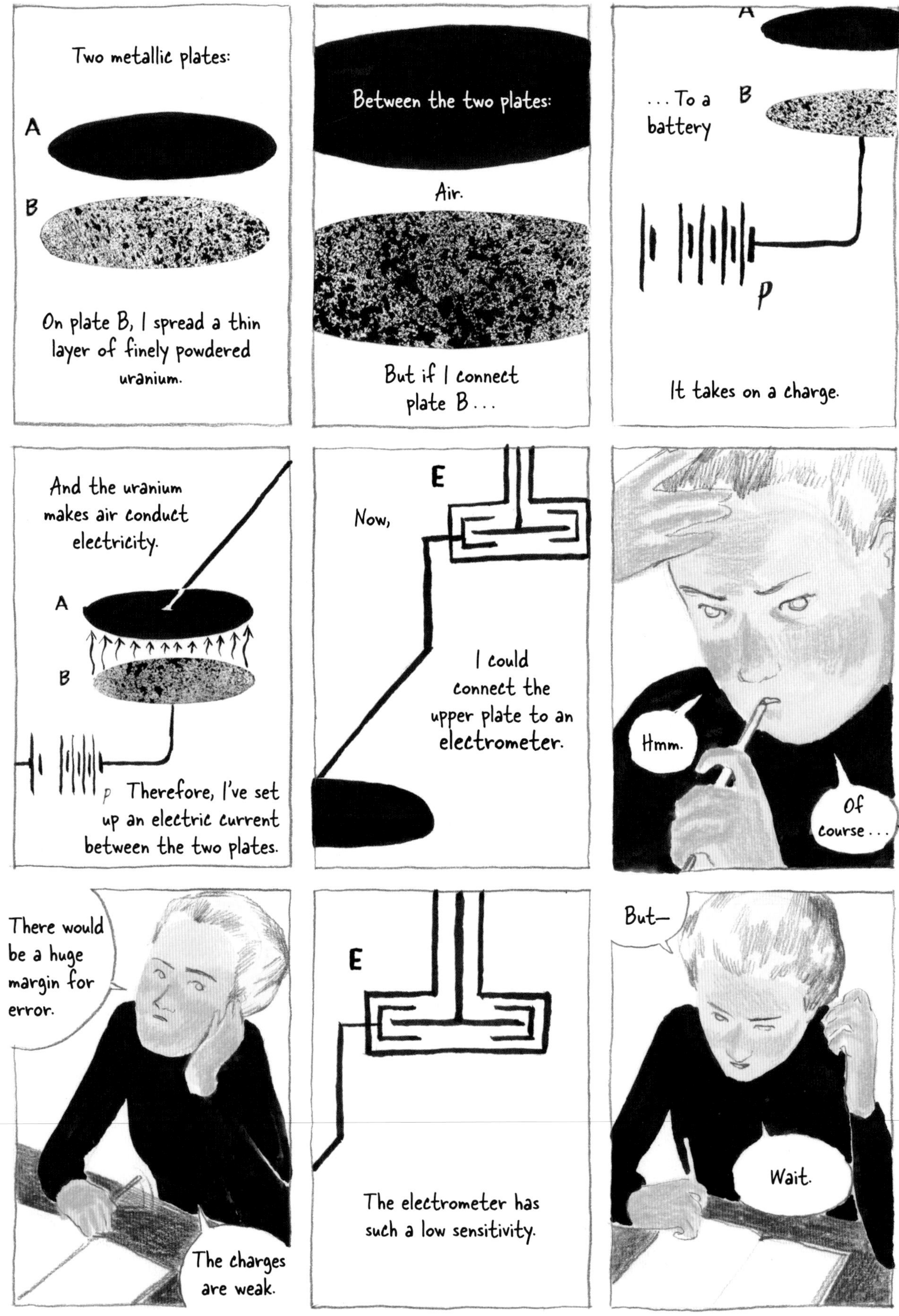
Two metallic plates:
A
B
On plate B, I spread a thin layer of finely powdered uranium.
Between the two plates:
Air.
But if I connect plate B . . .
A
B
. . . To a battery
P
It takes on a charge.
And the uranium makes air conduct electricity.
A
B
P
Therefore, I've set up an electric current between the two plates.
E
Now,
I could connect the upper plate to an electrometer.
Hmm.
Of course . . .
There would be a huge margin for error.
The charges are weak.
E
The electrometer has such a low sensitivity.
But—
Wait.

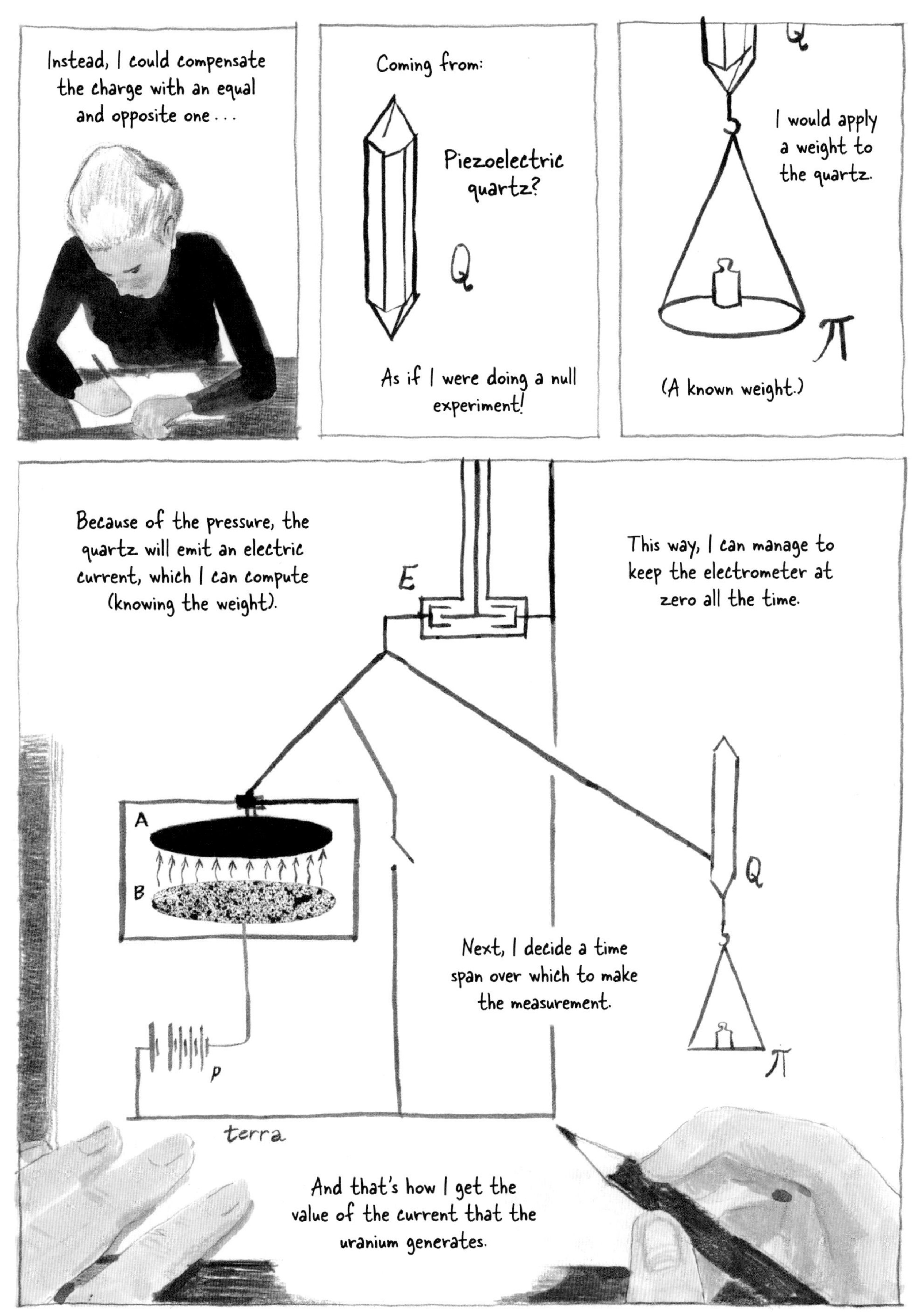
Instead, I could compensate the charge with an equal and opposite one . . .
Coming from:
Piezoelectric quartz?
Q
As if I were doing a null experiment!
I would apply a weight to the quartz.
π
(A known weight.)
Because of the pressure, the quartz will emit an electric current, which I can compute (knowing the weight).
E
This way, I can manage to keep the electrometer at zero all the time.
A
B
Q
Next, I decide a time span over which to make the measurement.
P
π
terra
And that's how I get the value of the current that the uranium generates.

I'll be able to measure the absolute value of the electric charge passing through the condenser at a given time..
And the measurement will be independent of the sensitivity of the electrometer.
E
Q
A
B
π
P
terra
The fact that these uranium rays leave impressions on the plates has been proven.
But what is their intensity?
How can the rays be constant? How can they never lose their charge?

What is their origin?
Energy can neither be created nor destroyed.
That's the first law of thermodynamics.

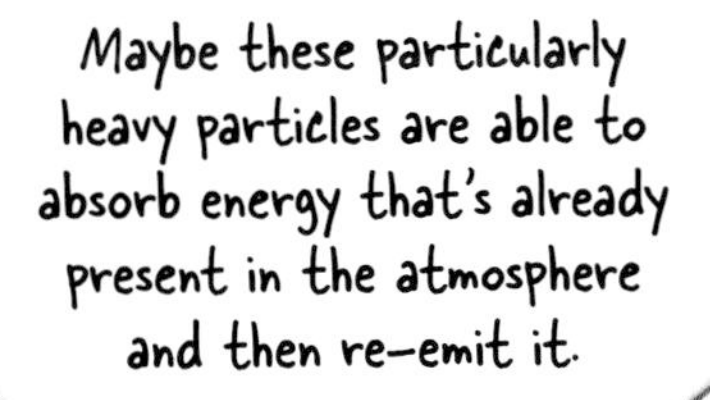
Maybe these particularly heavy particles are able to absorb energy that's already present in the atmosphere and then re-emit it.
Or is it a force coming from inside the atom of uranium itself?

Hmm . . .

First things first—I need some samples.

My father, Alexandre-Edmond Becquerel, has been studying phosphorescence for a long time.
Your father was a scientist too, Henri?
Of course! My grandfather as well.

Both honored members of the Academy of Sciences.
I see . . .
Phosphorescence has always sparked my imagination.
This uranium, though . . . stunning.
I know. I've read all of your works.
And now you need minerals.
Is that right?

I'm studying the conductivity of air under the influence of the uranium rays that you discovered.
I'd like to find out whether other substances besides uranium are able to make air conduct electricity.
Ah! Very interesting!
Then you're in the right place!

This is a sample of torbernite. Isn't it marvelous?
And this one?
It's pitchblende. It comes from Joachimsthal, in Austria.
Hmmm . . .
Pitchblende.
The director is a dear friend of mine. He would be happy to lend it to you for scientific purposes.

E
Q
A
B
PARIS,
1898

I examined a number of metals, salts, oxides, and minerals.

All the uranium compounds I studied are active. In general, the more uranium they contain, the more active they are.

However, two uranium minerals are much more active than the uranium itself: pitchblende (a uranium oxide) and chalcolite (uranyl copper phosphate).

That's most remarkable,
and it leads me to think
that these minerals may
contain an element much
more active than uranium.

BUT HOW!?
MOUTARDE de dijon
Want some on yours?
Yes, please.
So I'm saying, how is it possible?
No composite mineral could be more active than uranium!
Indeed!
There must be another element mixed in those compounds that's more active than uranium.
ANOTHER ELEMENT?

Are you sure?
How can we identify it?
We?
If you agree to it, Marie, I would like to offer my help.
But, Pierre!
However small.
What about your crystal research?

The crystals can wait.
Oh, Pierre!
If we find it...
If we can isolate it, and it actually is a new element...
I...
...Would like to name it polonium.
Sure, why not?
Polonium.
Sounds good, right?

Hey, Jean!
Look, the Curies!
Always cooing at each other.
Actually, we were talking about work.
Have a seat!
Want some salami?
I can make you a sandwich.
No thanks, I ate.
Some guys are unloading a truck over there.
They say they're from Austria.
IT ARRIVED!
Yes, but watch out! That Schulz is a nervous character!
My pitchblende!

WOULD YOU LIKE TO EXPLAIN TO ME WHAT THIS IS ALL DOING HERE?

GRAVEL IN THE COURTYARD OF THE INSTITUTE?!

It's not gravel, Director Schulz. It's extraction residue from uranium mining.

NOBODY HAS AUTHORIZED YOU TO LEAVE THIS JUNK ALL OVER THE COURTYARD!!
Excuse me?
JUNK??
EXCUSE ME VERY MUCH IF I ATTEMPT TO OBTAIN THE MATERIALS FOR MY RESEARCH. OH HOW BRAZEN I WAS! WELL, IF IT BOTHERS YOU SO MUCH THAT I'M TESTING THESE TONS OF PITCHBLENDE HERE, WITH MY HANDS...
All right, Marie! Don't get so bent out of shape!
GIVE ME THE MONEY TO GET IT DONE IN A DAMN FACTORY!!

I'm only saying that this stuff can't stay in the courtyard.
We can't boil the pitchblende in our little room. It creates too much smoke!
Nobody can breathe!
What about the old anatomy classroom? It's huge!
You'd have as much space as you like.
It's well lit, well ventilated . . .
Ventilated in the sense that there isn't any glass on the windows?
HERE'S THE BOTTOM LINE.

DEAL

WITH IT!!

NOTES
My current work presents the research I have carried out for more than four years on radioactive substances.

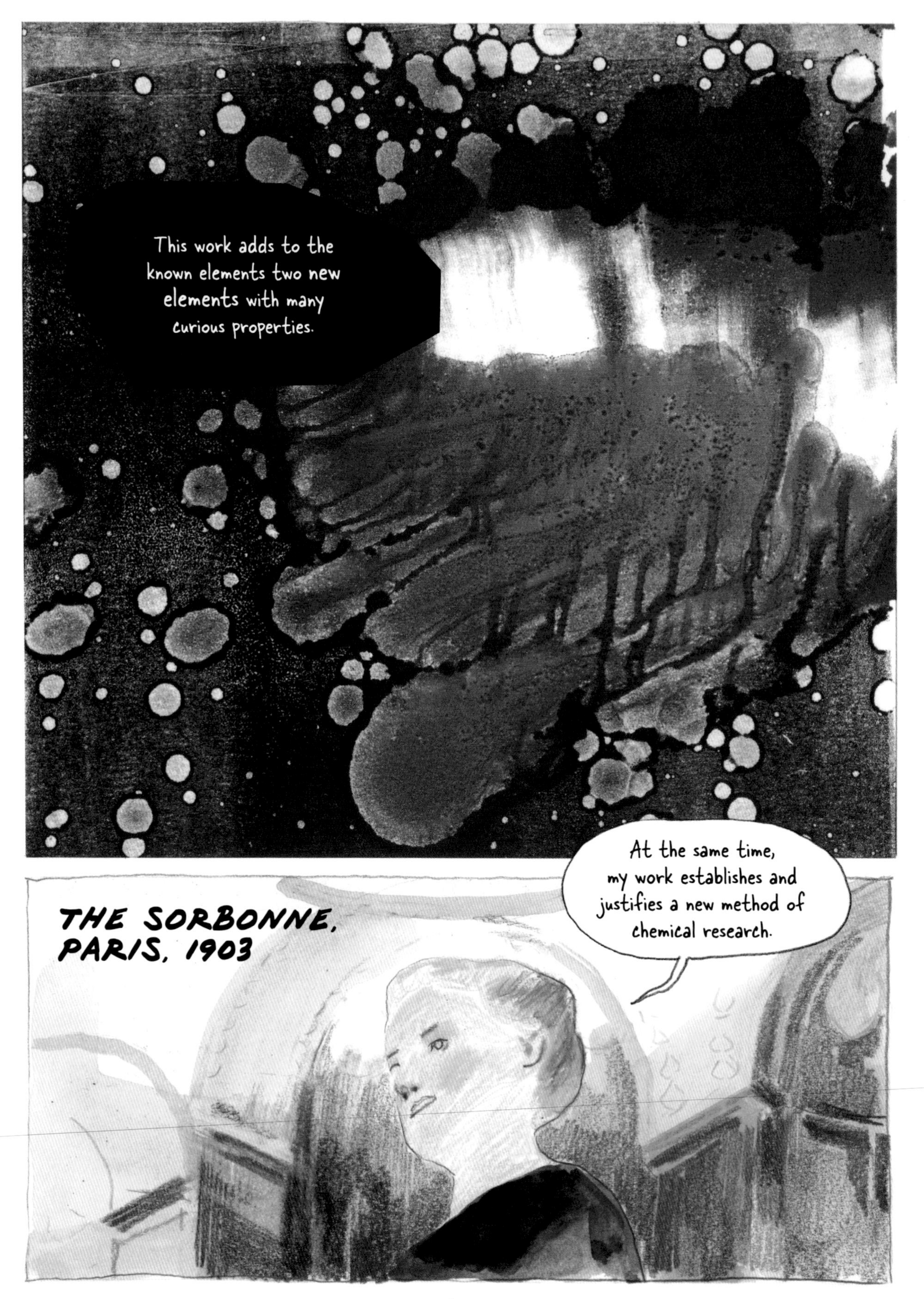
This work adds to the known elements two new elements with many curious properties.
THE SORBONNE, PARIS, 1903
At the same time, my work establishes and justifies a new method of chemical research.

The method could be based only on radioactivity, since we know of no other property of the hypothetical new substances.
Here is how one can use radioactivity to pursue this kind of research:
The radioactivity of a compound is measured.

A chemical decomposition is carried out on the compound.
The radioactivity of all of the obtained products is measured.
One then determines if the radioactive substance . . .
. . . has remained totally within one of the producs . . .
Or whether it is distributed among the obtained products, and in what proportions.

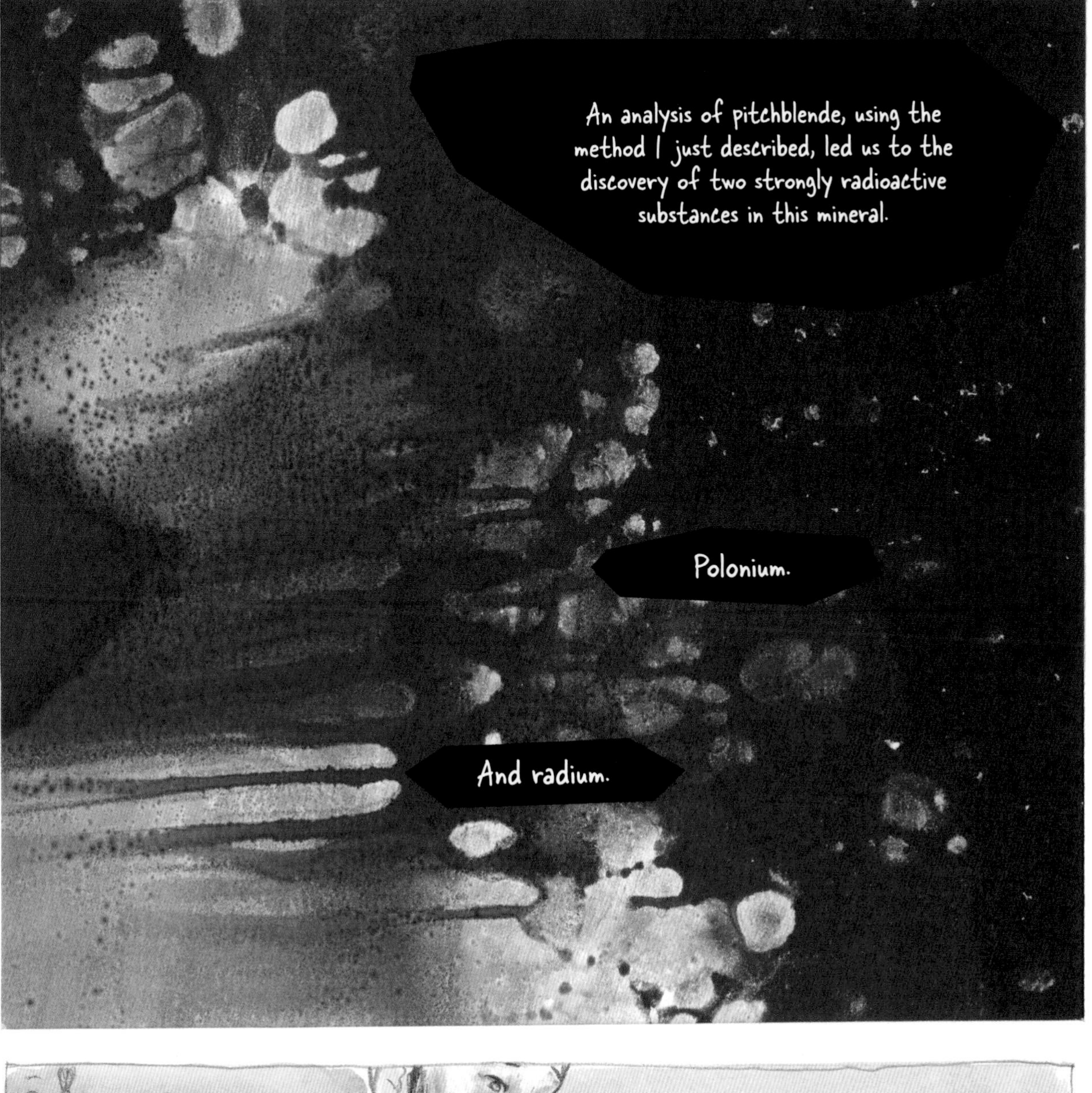
An analysis of pitchblende, using the method I just described, led us to the discovery of two strongly radioactive substances in this mineral.
Polonium.
And radium.

Shhh!
Poland!
Mama discovered Poland!
Polonium, from an analytical point of view, is a substance similar to bismuth.

Radium is a substance that resembles barium and it accompanies it in its reactions.

It separates from barium because of the different solubility of its chlorides in water.

These new radioactive bodies occur in quite infinitesimal amounts in pitchblende.

To obtain the elements in a more concentrated state, we had to treat several tons of uranium mining waste. This harsh treatment was followed by a process of purification and concentration.

We were thus able to extract from thousands of kilograms of raw material . . .

A few decigrams of products...

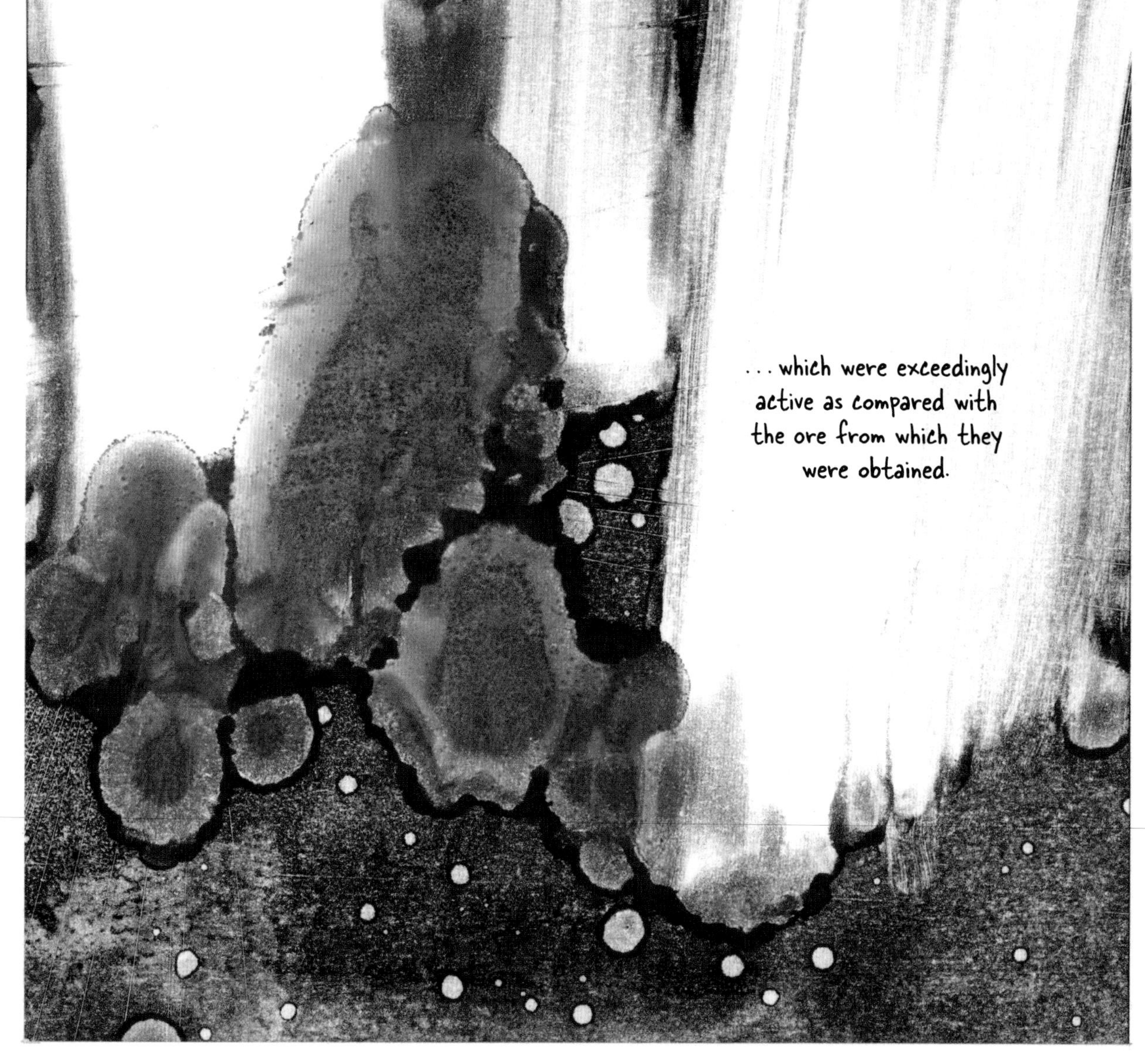
...which were exceedingly active as compared with the ore from which they were obtained.

A TOAST TO MARIE CURIE, DOCTOR OF SCIENCE!
WHOOO!
CONGRATULATIONS!
HIP HIP HOORAY!
CHEERS!
Congratulations, Marie!
Thank you, Jean!
May your future be as radiant as the substance you have discovered.
And thank you to Paul Langevin for organizing this great party!
My pleasure!
Marie, I wanted to give you my compliments. The work you have done is . . .
CRACK!
??
OH, DAMN IT!!
Uh—
Please excuse me . . .

Dunno.
What's happening?
LOOK WHAT HAPPENED! MY BEAUTIFUL SOUP BOWL!
I'm sorry!
Forgive me!
I'm sorry!
Jeanne, what happened?
What's all this screaming?
LOOK!
I'm mortified . . .
YOUR SCIENTIST FRIENDS BROKE MY MOTHER'S SOUP BOWL!!
ALL THESE PEOPLE IN MY HOUSE ARE GETTING ON MY NERVES.
Jeanne, calm down now.
Lower your voice . . .
Don't be difficult, please.
At least not today!
WHEN ARE THEY ALL GOING TO GO AWAY??

THEY'RE NOT JUST PEOPLE.
THEY'RE MY FRIENDS.
OH REALLY?
GO TO HELL! YOU AND THEM.
I'M SICK OF COOKING.
SLAM!

Marie!
Come here for a second? There's someone I want you to meet!
Ernest Rutherford.
He's passing through Paris.
Very pleased to meet you.
Congratulations. Your presentation was impeccable, and I really admire your research.

Thank you!
And you know . . .
I'm also doing research on radioactive material.
Of course.
I know!
Pierre and I have read all of your articles.
Including the one about the theory of transmutation.
Mama!
And . . . ?
What did you think?
I don't know . . .
Too soon to say with certainty. It's definitely intriguing.
What is it?
What's the theory of tramputation?
Transmutation, Irène.

Explain it to Irène.
She's a curious child. Interested in science.
Oh, well . . .
What did you say her name is?
Irène.
See, Irène . . .
The radium atom, which is made up of many little balls . . .
Loses one little ball.
It shoots it away very quickly . . .
And every ball that's shot away produces a lot of energy.
Energy?
Yes.
Heat, electricity . . . it's called radiation.
Afterwards, the radium is a little bit lighter.
I understand. Because it lost a little piece.
Exactly. And after it has lost a few balls . . .

. . . The radium isn't even radium anymore.
It has become something else, a completely different element: radon, which has a slightly lower atomic weight than the radium.
It's a little lighter?
Yes.
But radon is also nice and radioactive. Did you know that?
It also shoots little balls and emits energy.
It transforms.
Then you have polonium.
And so on . . .
Polonium!
That's what Mommy found!
Until one fine day . . .

Polonium is so tired from losing pieces of itself and energy...
That it becomes lead.
Which is inert.
That means it no longer emits anything.
Oooh!
Poor thing...
Thank the gentleman for the explanation, Irène.
Go play in the backyard with your father.
Did you see that? I convinced her!
Because it's perfectly logical!

Yes . . .
It's very nice your idea's logical.
But is it also true?
You come up with a complex theory and then hope that experiments will support it.
Madame.
That which you call radiation . . .
. . . is alpha particles . . .
. . . expelled in the form of gas from an atom that is undergoing a transformation.
In fact . . .
I did a number of experiments on alpha particles.
But I found a way to count them, and do you know how many there are?
It took me months, years!
3.4×10^{10} particles expelled per second.
From one gram of radium.
A-ha . . .

Then I deduced their mass.
From that I can calculate the weight of the next element in the transformation chain.
Which just happens to be . . .
. . . the exact weight of radon!
Yes, but you don't have any proof.
According to our experiments, radioactivity remains constant.
And the weight of the substance does not decrease.
I'll find an experiment that proves the opposite.
It's just a matter of time.
Ah, here you are!
I measure first.
Then I speak.
Madame Curie!
Tell me . . .
Is it true that radiation will cure baldness and light up the streets?
That's . . quite unlikely.

Children, come here!
No . . .
Here.
Where it's darker.
I'll show you something . . .
AAAH!
OOOOOOOOOHHH!
OOH!!
WHAT IS IT?
It's the light of the future!

WHAA!!
Can we touch it?
It also colors the glass of the tube, see?
Pierre!
Of course!
Pierre, hurry!
What is it?
Oh God!
Marie fainted!

This is happening a lot these days...
It's because of her thesis work.
She's so pale!
Her pulse is weak.
Is she eating enough?

No.
Maybe her blood pressure is low.
This isn't happening because she's overworked.
What are you saying?
Marie doesn't feel well because . . .
She's pregnant!
Pierre, you old dog, that's fantastic!
This demands a toast!
To your health!
Here, drink up.

Congratulations, Pierre and Marie!
To the unborn child—cheers!

The incident has so mortified me that I don't have the courage to write to anyone.

I had grown so used to the idea
of having this child . . .
I must admit, I did not
conserve my strength.

I trusted my robust health, and now I have paid dearly. I so regret it.
Shhhh!
Not now, Irène!
How are you?
I brought you the mail.
Should I open it?

Who's this?
Christopher Aurivillius . . .
. . . Secretary of the Royal Swedish Academy?
Ah—ha.
It seems that we have won the Nobel Prize.
Along with Becquerel.
What?
They're asking us to deliver a lecture in Stockholm.
In December.
December??
Are they crazy??
It's going to be freezing! And I'm not sure if I'm completely recovered!

You're right, Marie. I'll respond by thanking them . . .
And I'll say that we can come to Sweden in the New Year.
Maybe around Easter.
Don't worry, my love.
Just rest.

Le Petit Journal, one franc, everyone!
Stockholm honors amazing discovery!
Here you go.
Le Petit Journal
SENSATIONAL FRENCH DISCOVERY REWARDED IN STOCKHOLM.
His ASSISTANT!?
Mr. Pierre Curie
Mr. Becquerel
Also recognized was Pierre Curie's assistant, Maria
kłodowska Curie, his pupil at ESPCI and then
s bride. Following the ceremonies in Stockh
Petit Journal spoke with Mrs. Skłodo
e about her husband's status
reeminent researcher

"Of course!" the delicate woman answers, waving her hands with emotion. "And don't you think you deserve to be given a professorship as well, or membership in the Academy of Sciences?"

I can't believe it . . .

Marie, they claim you answered like this: "Oh no! I'm just a woman! My only joy is to help my husband with his research!"

It's a lie!

I'm going to write a letter to the newspaper.

Mrs. Skłodowska Curie (of Polish descent but French by adoption) is a devoted scientific collaborator of her husband and has attached her name to his discoveries.
But can a woman be part of the world's scientific elite and still maintain the delicate feelings of a wife and mother?
Is the modern woman on the verge of abandoning her traditional role in the home to devote herself to studies that, until now, were a man's territory?

A woman who works by definition neglects her home and her children.
We can only imagine the terrible consequences for the psyches of these children.
Little Irène, for example, must have been forced to eat in total solitude so that her mother could win the Nobel Prize.
Mommy doesn't love me anymore!

How is this possible?
And how'd this crazy idea of a nomination for the Academy of Sciences come up?
As if I need the recognition of those old windbags.
Tsk.
They must have come by the house when I wasn't here.
The only thing I need is a decent laboratory.
Pierre . . .
Think about it.
A position with the Academy of Sciences would bring you many advantages . . .
Including the funds for a laboratory.
Don't underestimate it.
Pff . . .
Look, all this politicking . . .
I don't understand it.
These strategies to gain something . . .

They're just power struggles, and I want to stay out of them.
I'm only interested in doing research.

Marie?
Oh!
You're so beautiful.

How does it look?
Great!
But it's absurd.
Why?
It cost an arm and a leg.
For one stupid dress, that's ridiculous!
Come now, it's just one time.
It suits you so well!
Hm.
All right.
Are you ready?
Yes.
You?
Irène?
Are you nervous?
Are you dressed yet?
Let's go!

FRENCH ACADEMY OF SCIENCES PARIS, 1905

After the proclamation at the Academy, we moved to a larger house with a garden. We did not go to Sweden that spring.
You, Pierre, were suffering from muscular pain, rheumatism, neurasthenia . . . That's what the doctors said. But they didn't understand. You had trouble moving, working.

We went to Sweden the following year, when your health had improved.

It was the month of June.
Remember how beautiful it was?
So bright! And the ride in the boat . . .
I was pregnant again.

This time, everything went well.

The birth of Ève helped me shake off all the bad memories.

We spent that summer in Normandy. My sister came from Poland with her daughter.

Do you remember? We saw the eclipse . . .

You bought the smoked glass for the little girls. They were delighted!

We were happy. I was convinced nothing could trouble us.

We said our goodbyes at the station.

Pierre.
My Pierre.

I will never
have enough tears
to cry.

PARIS, 1909
I am no longer able to devote myself to a life of relationships.

I don't see friends unless it's for work reasons or for the education of the children.

Nobody comes to visit me, and I don't see anyone.
Some in the laboratory have been offended by me. They haven't found me friendly enough.

They offered me your post, Pierre.
I've accepted.
BOUQINS

Some fools have even congratulated me.

You would be pleased to see me as a professor at the Sorbonne.

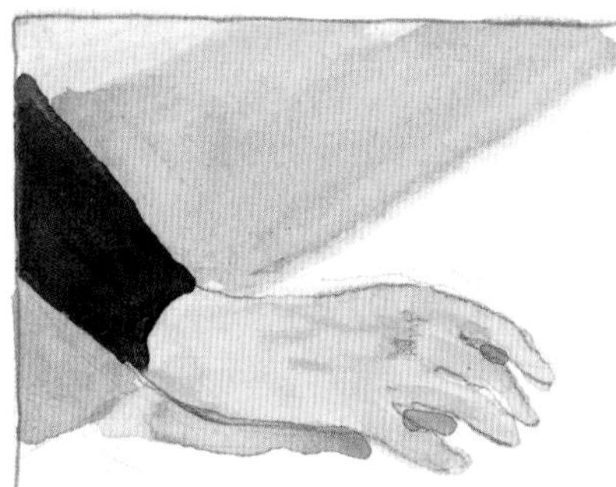

But to take your place, Pierre . . .

I have the feeling that the ability
to truly live is dead in me.

I no longer feel any vitality,
no spark of youth.

I no longer know what
joy or pleasure is.

Tomorrow I'll be
39 years old.

I may not have much time to
finish the work we started.

How sweet it would be to go to sleep and not wake up.
My little girls are so young.
I am so tired!

Marie?

Oh, hi, Marguerite.
What are you doing here all by yourself?
How are you?
You know...
You're pale.
Do you feel all right?
It's nothing...
I was just going home.
I'll walk with you!
...No, thank you.
Don't be silly! It's on my way!
No, Marguerite, really.
I'll go by myself, thanks.
But...
You're very kind, but there isn't anything you can do for me now.
Oh!
...

In this case, each element of a must also be an element of b, and vice versa . . .
scritch
scritch
scritch
scritch
Where b is the set of numbers that can be divided by 4.
Understand?
Mmm . . .
Yes.
Yes, yes.
?

And this was set theory.
Well!
I'd say we're finished for the day.
Hi, Marie!
Mama!
Hi, Paul. Hi, kids.
Put your notebook away before you get up, Irène.
Hi, Marie!
Good morning, Marie!
Good morning!
Morning, Marie!
Hey, Marie!
Before the physics lesson, let's all go out in the courtyard—it's a beautiful day!
Yeah!
Yes!
Yay!

How are you, Marie?
Tired, Paul. Very tired.
But what can I do . . . ?
And you?
Marguerite told me she ran into you.
Tonight we're all going to her house.
The Perrins will be there too.
Would you like to come?
Let's go!
Everybody outside. Come on!
Bye, Madame Curie!

I don't know, Paul.
Frankly, I don't have the urge to be around other people.

But, Marie!
Why are you doing this?
It would do you good to spend a little time with us . . .
At the end of the day, we're your friends.
That's why we're here.
Hm . . .
Maybe you're right.
So you'll come?
Yes.
Live a little, right?
Great!

Marie!
What a lovely dress.

Paul, my friend . . .
I spent the evening and night yesterday thinking of you and of the hours we have spent together.

It would be so nice to be free to see each other when our schedules allow it.
There are true affinities between us that only require some favorable conditions to develop.
We are bound by a deep affection, and we must not allow it to be destroyed.

PIG!!

DISGUSTING PIG! HOW COULD YOU? WITH THAT INFAMOUS ROMANIAN?
She's Polish.
How did you get those?

IF ANY PART OF THIS BECOMES PUBLIC
I'LL SPIT YOUR NAME ALL OVER PARIS!!
THIS'LL CAUSE A SCANDAL...
Give me back my letters.
OW!!
It's a scientific correspondence!
I'LL RUIN YOU!!!

LOOK WHAT YOU DID!
MY POOR SON... YOUR PIG OF A FATHER
HAS A MISTRESS!

Paul!
Good lord.
What happened to you?
Hi, Emile, Marguerite . . .
Oh, Jean, Henriette, you came too! Thank you.
Is it true that she threatened to kill Marie?
What?
???
Yes, and she could do it too.

Oh, Jean, what a mistake . . .
What a huge mistake my marriage was.
I've thought a thousand times about getting a divorce.
But . . . the kids.
Hang on a minute.
Do you think seeing you two fight and throw dishes at each other is good for their growth?
How do you figure?
You think they'll grow up happy like that?
FINE!
BUT WHAT CAN I DO?

Jeanne has the letters.
She threatened to give them to the newspapers.
She wants me to renounce custody of the children.
And she wants me to pay 1,000 francs in alimony.
Otherwise, she'll publish them.
SHE'S BLACKMAILING YOU??
And she absolutely wants Marie to leave France.
And go back to Poland.
What?
Her life is here now!
Her children are French!
Go back to Poland?
Everyone—
Let's be reasonable.

Every husband in France has a mistress nowadays.

A modest young girl that he sees discreetly. Whom he supports.

The fact here is that Marie is a woman with a brilliant career, with ideas . . .

And personal aspirations.

That's why Marie is trouble.

Tsk.
Jeanne's using the kids as a bargaining chip.
She's a snake!
Indeed!
But what will people say?
Oh, that poor mother in tears! Defending hearth and home . . .
And she's ready to forgive her husband's escapades, as long as he returns to the fold.
But for Heaven's sake, don't take her children from her!
Her only consolation.

That's Jeanne.
The perfect French woman.
And Marie is a black sheep, too emancipated, with her masculine aspirations . . .
. . .
It makes me sick.
These double standards, this caveman mind-set!
Out of date.
Medieval.
Calm down, Marguerite. Let's . . .
Regressive but respectable!
. . .

The agreement is that she won't publish the letters as long as I stop seeing Marie.
Except...
Except?

The Solvay Congress.
We've both been invited.
It's in Brussels.
Well, but that's work, right?

BRUSSELS,
BELGIUM, 1911

Madame Curie . . .
Founder, after receiving the Nobel Prize, of the prestigious Institut du Radium in Paris.
METROPOLE
She was the first to isolate radium and determine its atomic weight.

And it is to her that this commission has decided to entrust the task . . .
. . . of preparing a sample that will act as an international unit of radioactivity.
It will be called Curie, in honor of Pierre . . .

. . . who left us seven years ago.

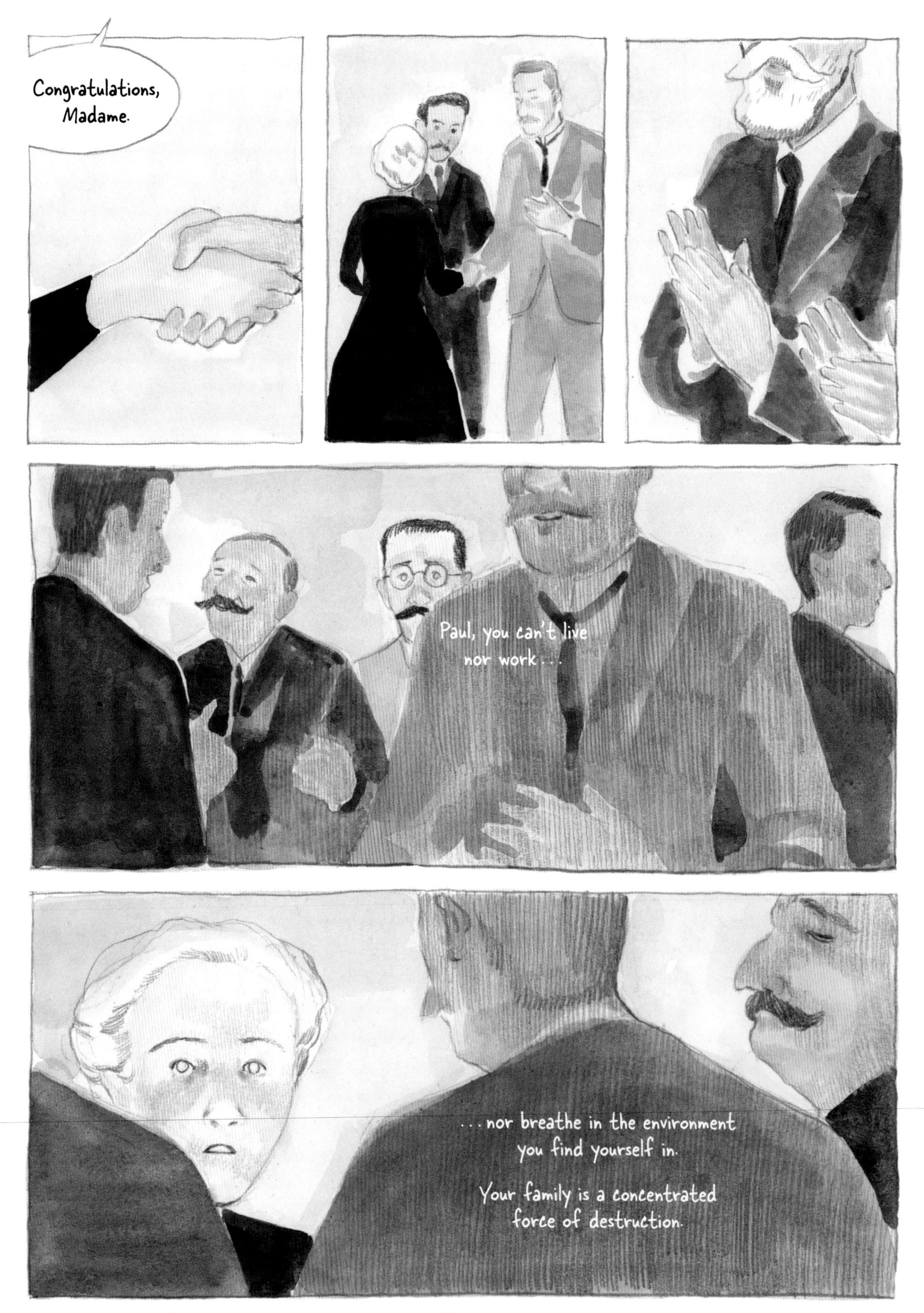
Congratulations, Madame.
Paul, you can't live nor work . . .
. . . nor breathe in the environment you find yourself in.
Your family is a concentrated force of destruction.

Jeanne is too accustomed to using violence to manipulate you. She doesn't even realize the harm she's causing her children.

She will not accept a separation easily either.

It would be against her interests. After all, she has always lived off your money.

She will pressure you to get her pregnant again, and I wouldn't be able to stand that.

You have to be wary of this.

You must separate your beds. Please don't make me wait too long for your decision.

LE JOURNAL
ELOPEMENT
Mme. Curie and Professor Langevin
The wife is in tears:
"He destroyed our family."
Robbery with Chloroform on the Railways
The truth is that very deliberately, methodically, and scientifically, Mme. Curie has devoted herself, with the most treacherous methods, to removing a family man from his wife and to separate the wife from her children. All this emerges in their letters.
This foreigner claims to speak in the name of happiness and personal fulfillment. But is this true happiness when it goes against the most sacred of institutions?

Come in!
Oh, Ève! My, how you've grown!
There was an angry mob in front of Marie's house.
It was horrible.

Where is it?
Ah, here it is! On page 16.
"Madame Curie, weakened by the cruel misfortunes we are all aware of, nonetheless received warm congratulations from her admirers in Stockholm and Paris."
Oh, Marie!
Another Nobel. Congratulations!
This news will make up for all the slander of the past few months.
Thank you, dear, but I doubt it.
You can stay here with us until the waters are calmer.
Marguerite, Emile.
I... don't want to cause problems.
Don't even say that!
We're your friends. We have to protect you.

Pierre?

Marie!
I have to tell you . . .
I did an amazing experiment! Did you know that radium bromide . . .
. . . kept in a vacuum for three months, spontaneously emits gas?
It's helium!
I examined it, and it's absolutely helium.
Really?
Yes.
Do you remember Rutherford?
He was right.
Radiation is a gas. It's the product of the transformation of an atom.
Only it's such a slow process that we can't perceive the loss of weight.
We never noticed it.

So he was right?
Yes.
I miss talking to you, Pierre.

PARIS, 1936

When Marguerite's father discovered that she and Emile were hosting my mother in their apartment, he was furious.

Marguerite's father was the rector of the university in Paris.

"We've learned about some letters that concern you. Are they true? I can't believe it. Yet that seems to be the case. In any event, I caution you against accepting the Nobel Prize before you've clarified your situation."

That's what Secretary Aurivillius wrote.

But our mother went to Stockholm anyway.

The Nobel Prize is given in recognition for my scientific work, which has no relation to my private life.
That was her answer.

A few days after her return from Sweden, she was hospitalized.
She was very sick.
She had lesions on her kidneys. They said she was anemic.

...
It was a strange form of anemia that couldn't be explained. She was convalescing for almost two years.

What about Langevin?

They maintained a working relationship.
Vaguely friendly.

But very, very detached.

In the end, he went back to his wife.

And do you know what's crazy?

A few years later, he already had another mistress.

A secretary.

Certainly.

It's a shame.
After Father died, she still could have been happy.
Instead . . .
. . .
Well, then the Great War came.
Nobody cared about the scandal anymore.
Marie could be useful.
She set up a battalion of radiology machines. She trained thousands of nurses on how to use them.

Including me.
And me?
You were in Britain with the Polish governess.
You were too young.
Ah.
Wow.
Quite an impressive story.

Oh!
Did we tell you about the time we went to America with my mother to pick up a gram of radium—
From the hands of President Harding.
Yes, I told him about that.
Your family is a gold mine of anecdotes.
I hope I get to know them all one day.
You'll get sick of them long before you hear them all, dear.
Okay, we're going out.
Goodbye, Madame Irène.
Ève, that's quite a neckline!
Come on!
Have fun.

It was radiation that caused my mother's strange anemia.
As we now know.
My parents just thought it only made superficial burns on the skin.

Who could have imagined that it would have such profound physiological effects?
Who could have suspected everything that came later?

Thank you for everything, Mother.
Thank you, Father.

I WISH YOU WERE
HERE NOW.

The Legacy of Marie

by Alberto Anselmi, Andrea Milani, and Anna Nobili

In central Paris, near Rue d'Ulm, sat the Institut du Radium, founded in 1909 and built for Marie Curie between 1911 and 1914 as an initiative of the University of Paris and the Institut Pasteur. The Institut du Radium consisted of two buildings separated by a small garden. The Curie laboratory was dedicated to researching the chemistry and physics of radioactivity, and the Pasteur laboratory was dedicated to its medical and biological applications. With this space, Curie finally had a laboratory worthy of her talents (and her fame, after two Nobel Prizes!). She directed the studies at the Cure laboratory until her death in 1934.

Marie Curie, pictured here in 1906, influenced the study of radioactivity both through her scientific findings and through her role at the Institut du Radium, a research complex developed in the decade after her 1903 receipt of the Nobel Prize in Physics.

The two laboratories embraced the vast inheritance of Marie Curie's discoveries. The medical laboratory built on previous successes in using radiotherapy to treat cancer. Assisted by her daughter, Irène, Curie taught courses there for radiology nurses. In more recent times, the site has become an eight-story medical clinic. The physics and chemistry laboratory served as the seat of the research by Irène and her husband, Frédéric Joliot-Curie, on artificial radioactivity, for which they jointly received the Nobel Prize in 1935.

Marie and Pierre Curie had made an important contribution to science with the discoveries of radioactivity and the natural transmutation of the elements. The Joliot-Curies continued their work, demonstrating the possibility of artificially induced transmutations (the changing of one element into another). The key to understanding the new developments came in 1932, with British physicist James Chadwick's discovery of the neutron. Because the neutron had no electric charge, it could penetrate and hit an atomic nucleus, which absorbed it by reemitting radiation and creating the nucleus of a different element.

Italian physicist Enrico Fermi became the first person to announce a transmutation intentionally obtained by neutron irradiation. Starting in 1934, Fermi and his colleagues at the Institute of Physics in Rome bombarded the nuclei of various elements with neutrons. The nuclei reemitted particles and were transformed into nuclei of different elements, many of them radioactive. When Fermi repeated the experiment with nuclei of uranium (the heaviest element existing in nature), he interpreted the result as the creation of new "transuranic" elements—that is, even heavier than the original uranium nuclei. This became the prevailing interpretation, even if doubts remained.

In addition to Irène and Frédéric Joliot-Curie's research on the transmuation of elements, Lise Meitner and Otto Hahn in Berlin, Germany, were dedicated to the same subject. The history of this small group of scientists intertwines with the tragedies of World War II and anti-Semitism. Enrico Fermi and his colleagues in Rome dispersed when the Italian government's racial laws forced the group's Jewish members to take refuge abroad. In 1938 Fermi—whose wife was Jewish—used the occasion of a trip to Stockholm to receive the Nobel Prize to flee to the United States with his family.

Meitner, a Jewish researcher from Vienna (then of Austria-Hungary, later of Austria) studied physics despite great difficulties. At the turn of the twentieth century, women were not typically admitted to Austria's universities. Nonetheless Meitner was among the first women in Austria to receive a doctorate in physics. After moving to Berlin, Meitner met Hahn, a talented chemist with whom she established a scientific collaboration that lasted thirty years. Although Meitner's Jewish heritage made her time in Germany fraught, her Austrian citizenship protected her from harm until Hitler's annexation of Austria in 1938. She was forced to leave Berlin but, with the help of Hahn and other colleagues, she managed to settle in Stockholm, Sweden.

Hahn and Meitner conducted experiments along the same lines as those of the researchers in Paris and Rome. They too were convinced they were working with transuranic elements (artificially made radioactive elements with atomic numbers higher than uranium). However, at the end of 1938, following an experiment published by Irène Joliot-Curie, Hahn demonstrated that the product of the reaction of neutron hitting a uranium nucleus was barium, an element whose atomic weight was *half* that of uranium. This was the first experimental evidence of fission.

Hahn informed Meitner of the results of the experiment right away. Meitner soon produced, in collaboration with Otto Frisch, a physical model of the reaction. The model predicted the energies these reactions produced to be much larger than those usually produced in chemical reactions. Many similar experiments in Europe and the United States verified this prediction. A few years later, in 1945, Hahn received the Nobel Prize in Chemistry as a result of this research. Some of the most respected scientists of the time, such as Niels Bohr, proposed a parallel award in physics for Meitner and Frisch, but the proposal was not accepted. Meanwhile, Frédéric Joliot-Curie had been able to describe the chain reaction involving a mass of uranium whereby the emission of energy would become a macroscopic fact. Thus, at the dawn of World War II, the possibility of producing nuclear energy, both in controlled form and as a massive explosion, became clear to nuclear scientists in many countries.

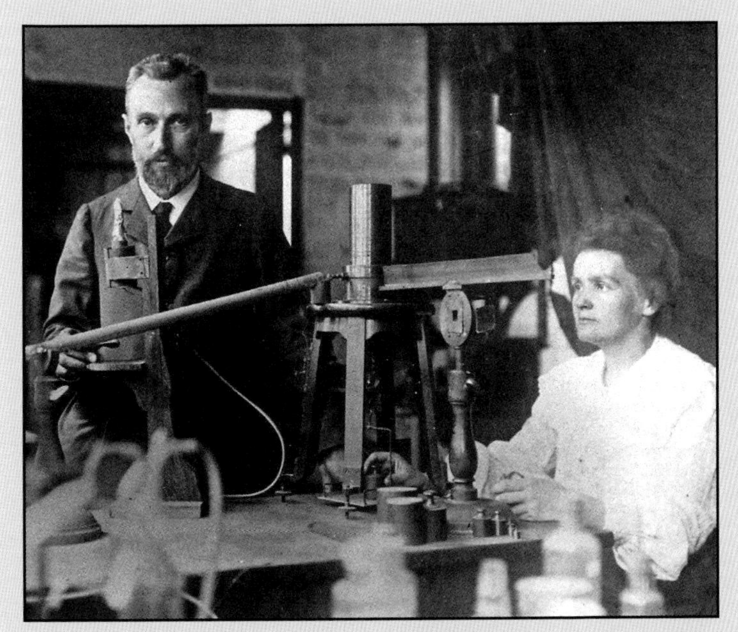

In the years after Pierre Curie and Marie Curie (seen here in 1904) made their contributions to physics and chemistry, their daughter Irène Joliot-Curie continued their work, further exploring the transmutation of elements alongside her husband, Frédéric Joliot-Curie.

On August 2, 1939, theoretical physicist Albert Einstein, solicited by physicist Leo Szilard, signed a letter to US president Franklin Delano Roosevelt. The letter warned Roosevelt that following the discoveries of Joliot-Curies, Szilard. and Fermi, nations could conceivably build bombs of enormous power (and that similar developments were likely to be taking place in Germany). In 1942 the United States centralized its research on nuclear fission in a single organization: the Manhattan Project. This organization included both

American physicists and refugee scientists from Europe. In July of 1945, in the New Mexico desert, the first test of a real atomic bomb took place.

That year Szilárd drafted a petition—signed by seventy scientists of the Manhattan Project—asking that an atomic bomb not be used on a civilian population. Despite the petition, on August 6, 1945, President Harry S. Truman decided to launch a bomb on the city of Hiroshima to induce the surrender of Japan. On August 9, 1945, the United States launched a second, even more powerful bomb on the Japanese city of Nagasaki. On August 15, Emperor Hirohito of Japan announced the nation's surrender.

While the European scientists who immigrated to the United States gave life to the atomic bomb and the Manhattan Project, the Joliot-Curies continued their research in Paris. In 1940 the Nazi invasion of France forced them to suspend their work, although they had shipped documentation and equipment to England. Frédéric then took part in the anti-Nazi efforts of the French Resistance. In the post-war period, he became high commissioner for atomic energy in France, directing the construction of the first French nuclear reactor until 1950, when he was removed for political reasons.

After the war, while many key scientists passed away—including Albert Einstein, Enrico Fermi, and Irène Joliot-Curie between 1954 and 1956—China, France, Russia, the United Kingdom, and the United States openly amassed nuclear weapons. Later, these nations and others attempted to stop the spread of nuclear weapons through the Treaty on the Non-Proliferation of Nuclear Weapons (signed in 1968 and made effective in 1970), although the development of nuclear weapons has continued in some areas of the world.

The story of Marie Curie and her family interests and concerns us not only for the extraordinary mark they left on scientific and human history but also for the consequences of their discoveries. The scientific, technological, and social outcomes of nuclear physics are part of our lives, from the power plants that generate part of the energy we consume (and waste we don't know how to deal with) to the large research centers that have changed the way science is done. Military developments, which played a crucial role during World War II, still dominate international politics and will continue to influence the history of humanity—to what extent, we are unable to tell.

Alberto Anselmi was born in Genoa, Italy, in 1953 and works for the European aerospace company Thales Alenia Space on satellite missions for space geodesy, planetary exploration, and fundamental physics.

Andrea Milani was born in Florence in 1948 and died in 2018 while this book was in preparation. He taught mathematics at the University of Pisa, focusing on celestial mechanics, particularly the calculation of the orbits of asteroids.

Anna Nobili was born in 1949 in a small village in the province of Rieti, Italy. She teaches physics at the University of Pisa, working on space experiments in fundamental physics. She was among the first women admitted to study physics at the Scuola Normale Superiore di Pisa.

Timeline

1867 Maria Salomea Skłodowska is born in Warsaw, Poland, on November 7.

1873 Her father, Władysław Skłodowski, loses his position as a teacher but opens a boarding school.

1878 Her mother, Bronisława Skłodowski, dies on May 9.

1891 Maria begins her studies at the University of Paris, also known as the Sorbonne, in Paris, France.

1893 She is awarded a degree in physics and also receives a degree in mathematics one year later.

1895 She marries Pierre Curie on July 26. Wilhelm Röntgen detects X-rays.

1896 Henri Becquerel detects evidence of radioactivity after experiments with uranium salts.

1897 She gives birth to her daughter Irène.

1898 She uses the term *radioactivity* for the first time on April 12. Marie and Pierre Curie announce the discoveries of polonium and radium in July and December, respectively.

1903 Marie and Pierre Curie, along with Henri Becquerel, win the Nobel Prize in Physics.

1904 She gives birth to her daughter Ève.

1906 Pierre Curie dies on April 19. Marie Curie becomes the first female professor at the Sorbonne.

1910 She defines the curie, an international unit of radioactivity.

1911 She wins the Nobel Prize in Chemistry.

1914 The Radium Institute is built. World War I begins.

1934 Marie Curie dies on July 4 from aplastic anemia, a possible result of long-term exposure to radiation.

Selected Bibliography

A considerable amount of material about Marie Curie exists. Much of the information used for the writing of this graphic novel comes from *Marie Curie: A Life* by Susan Quinn, a biography released in the United States in 1995 (with an Italian edition in 1998 from Bollati Boringhieri). Some information was also taken from *Madame Curie*, the great biography by her daughter Ève Curie, which was released in Europe and the United States in 1937. (I found an English edition from 1943.) It was also useful to consult the autobiographical notes of Marie Curie herself, which can be found in her account of her husband's life, published in 1923 with the title *Pierre Curie*. In this text, Curie retraces her own life in addition to drawing a portrait of her husband. (A new Polish edition was published in 2017 by the Maria Skłodowska-Curie Museum of Warsaw.) Curie also wrote *La Radiologie et la Guerre* (1921), which told of her experience with radiological machines during World War I.

For scientific documentation, I consulted the Nobel lectures by Henri Becquerel (1903), Pierre Curie (1905), Ernest Rutherford (1908), and Marie Curie (1911); several articles taken from the journal *Comptes Rendus de l'Academie des Sciences*; and *Recherches sur les substances radioactives*, the doctoral thesis that Marie Curie presented to the Faculty of Sciences of Paris in 1903. These texts are available for download in their original languages.

Also very useful was the book *Great Experiments in Physics: Firsthand Accounts from Galileo to Einstein*, edited by Morris H. Shamos and first published by Holt, Rinehart, and Winston in 1959. Especially helpful were the chapters "X-rays" by Wilhelm Röntgen and "Natural Radioactivity" by Henri Becquerel. Another helpful text was the article "The Laboratory Notebooks of Pierre and Marie Curie and the Discovery of Polonium and Radium" by J. P. Adloff, which analyzes the notebooks of Pierre and Marie Curie in the crucial months of the discovery of radium.

Source Notes

16–19 Marie Skłodowska, letters to Józef Skłodowski, March–May 1887. Quoted in Ève Curie, *Madame Curie*, 1937.

20 Bronisława Skłodowska, letter to Marie Skłodowska, March 1890. Quoted in Curie.

24–26 Henri Poincaré, *Les Méthodes Nouvelles de la Mécanique Celeste* (Paris: Gauthier Villars, 1892–99), 1892–99.

51–54 Pierre Curie, letters to Marie Skłodowska, August-September 1894. Quoted in Susan Quinn, *Marie Cure: A Life (New York: Simon and Shuster, 1995).*

61–63 Henri Becquerel, "Sur les radiations émises par phosphorescence," *Notes aux Comptes-rendus de l'Académie des Sciences*, no. 122 (February 24, 1896): 420–421.

Becquerel, "Sur les radiations invisibles émises par les corps phosphorescents," *Notes aux Comptes-rendus de l'Académie des Sciences*, March 1, 1896, 501–502.

70–72 J. P. Adloff, "The Laboratory Notebooks of Pierre and Marie Curie and the Discovery of Polonium and Radium," *Czechoslovak Journal of Physics*, 1999.

Marie Curie, "Recherches sur les substances radioactives" (doctoral thesis pres., French Academy of Sciences, June 1903).

79–80 Marie Curie, "Rayons émis par les composés de l'uranium et du thorium," *Notes aux Comptes-rendus de l'Académie des Sciences*, no. 126 (April 12, 1898): 1101–03.

91–98 Curie, "Recherches sur les substances radioactives."

104–108 Ernest Rutherford, "The Chemical Nature of the Alpha Particles from Radioactive Substances" (Nobel Lecture, December 11, 1908).

108 Pierre Curie and Marie Curie, "Sur les corps radioactifs," *Notes aux Comptes-rendus de l'Académie des Sciences*, no. 134 (January 13, 1902): 85.

146–152 Marie Curie, diary entries, 1907, quoted in Quinn, *Marie Cure: A Life*.

163–164 Marie Curie, letter to Paul Langevin, published in *L'Oeuvre* (November 23, 1911), quoted in Quinn, *Marie Cure: A Life*.

180–181 Curie.

187 Pierre Curie and J. Dewar, "Examen des gaz occlus ou dégagés par le bromure de radium," *Notes aux Comptes-rendus de l'Académie des Sciences*, no. 138 (January 25, 1904): 190.

About the Author

Born in Pisa in 1986, Alice Milani has studied painting, engraving, and printing techniques in Turin, Italy and Brussels, Belgium. She was one of the founders of the La Trama collective, through which she created and distributed self-produced graphic novels until 2015. Her first book, *Wisława Szymborska, si dà il caso che io sia qui* (BeccoGiallo, 2015) is a tribute to the Polish poet and Nobel Prize winner. It has been translated into Polish. She next released *Tumulto* (Eris Edizioni, 2016), a story of travel and change, cocreated with Silvia Rocchi. In 2017 she began creating a new work of graphic fiction for BeccoGiallo.

Acknowledgments

I would like to thank my two scientific consultants—and parents—Anna Nobili and Andrea Milani, for helping me to further understand the fundamental concepts of nuclear physics and contributing, with their thorough editing, to the scientific accuracy of this work. I would also like to thank Lorenzo Ghetti and Matteo Lupetti for their reading and advice, and Alice Socal for translating the lines of Wilhelm Röntgen and his wife from German. And I must thank Michaela Osimo for suggesting the dream scene and for one thousand other valuable suggestions. Finally, with all my heart I would like to thank Alessandro Spada, who remains the best agent I could ever wish for.